TEACHER TROUBLE

Steve Barlow and Steve Skidmore

Illustrated by Alex L

Franklin Watts
First published in Great Britain in 2017 by The Watts Publishing Group

Credits
Executive Editor: Adrian Cole
Design Manager: Peter Scoulding
Cover Designer: Cathryn Gilbert
Illustrations: Alex Lopez

HB ISBN 978 1 4451 5373 5
PB ISBN 978 1 4451 5375 9
Library ebook ISBN 978 1 4451 5374 2

Printed in China.

MIX
Paper from responsible sources
FSC® C104740

Franklin Watts
An imprint of
Hachette Children's Group
Part of The Watts Publishing Group
Carmelite House
50 Victoria Embankment
London EC4Y 0DZ

An Hachette UK Company
www.hachette.co.uk

www.franklinwatts.co.uk

Lin
Danny
Sam

The headteacher has news for the class...
Mr Broad is ill.
You have a new teacher today.
Great! We can mess about!

I heard that!
You will all behave. We are not monsters here!

Some of us are.

This is...
Hello!
My name is
Mr Hunter.

He looks odd!
Yeah. Even for a teacher!

I can't wait to find out all about you.

“What does he mean?” asked Lin.

Sam shook his head. “No idea.”

Later that day...
Lunch time!
!
BUMP!

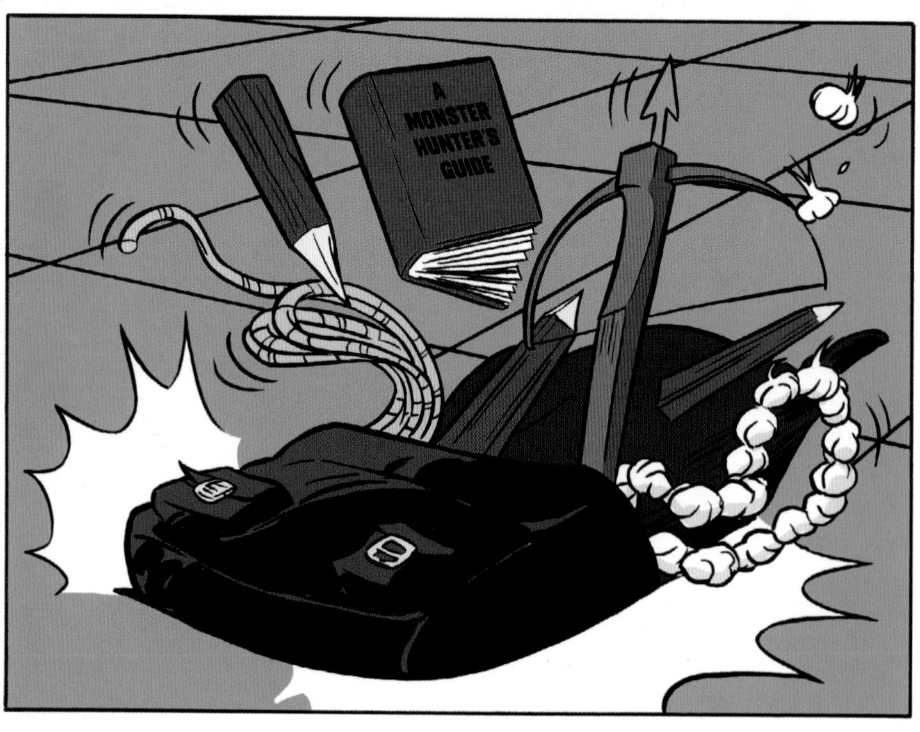
A MONSTER HUNTER'S GUIDE

I've got news
about Mr Hunter.
He has odd things
in his bag...

So have you, Sam. It's your smelly sports kit.

“What sort of things?” asked Clogger.

“Garlic, silver chains, salt, a bottle of holy water...”

Clogger laughed. “Maybe he’s a monster hunter! He’s come to take away the freaks.”

SPLURGE!

Danny, Lin and Sam were shocked.

"A monster hunter! What should we do?" asked Danny.

"What will he do to us?" asked Sam.

Silver! Noooo!

Salt!
Help!
Holy water!
Aaaargh!

“I have an idea. We should ask him if he is a monster hunter,” said Lin.

“Are you mad?” hissed Danny.

“No. Come on,” replied Lin.

“Hello. Can I help?” said Mr Hunter.

“We’ve heard a story... People say you are a monster hunter,” said Lin.

It's true. I am!
I can sense monsters at this school!

You're right! There is a monster!
I knew it!

It's Clogger. He's a real monster!
Leave him to me...

After lunch...
There is no escape! Show your true self!
A vampire?
No...

A werewolf?
No...
Then you must be a demon or zombie!

Argghhhh!!!

"What are you doing?" screamed the headteacher.

"There are monsters here!" said Mr Hunter.

"You are the only monster here!" replied the headteacher.

"Get out, now!"

Monsters here at Hangem High?
What a crazy idea!
THE END